FIREHEART URBAN FANTASY SHORT STORIES COLLECTION

CONNOR WHITELEY

No part of this book may be reproduced in any form or by any electronic or mechanical means. Including information storage, and retrieval systems, without written permission from the author except for the use of brief quotations in a book review.

This book is NOT legal, professional, medical, financial or any type of official advice.

Any questions about the book, rights licensing, or to contact the author, please email connorwhiteley@connorwhiteley.net

Copyright © 2021 CONNOR WHITELEY

All rights reserved.

DEDICATION
Thank you to all my readers without you I couldn't do what I love.

FELINE OF THE LOST

The dark yellow sand filled wind whipped across Tervis' face. Gently rubbing his skin bare with each gust of the desert wind.

He tried to pull up his dirty white tunic but he couldn't get it out under his cold metal armour. It was too tight.

The blowing wind continued to rub his face dry.

Trevis' hands formed fists in frustration. If only he had been better then he wouldn't have to deal with this desert.

So what, he might have been overly talkative, and he might have been deemed a danger to his fellow soldiers. But to give him a sentence of solitude and kicking him out of the army. That was harsh!

Trevis tried to forget about it and he kept putting one foot in front of the other. His large leather booted feet sinking into the rough yellow desert sand with each step. He could have sworn some sand had gotten into his boots from the stabbing sore pain that throbbed from his left foot.

Bravely, raising his head with his hands covering some of his eyes to protect them from the sand. He managed to see the desert landscape around him. With its short sand dunes and the sand relentlessly blowing everywhere.

He turned his head slightly and some sand got in his ears. Trevis screamed at the stupidity of this situation.

He didn't think getting kicked out the army would get his helmet taken from him. But apparently, it was 'in precious supply'.

Ridiculous!

Trevis had seen four new crates come to the main camp only yesterday.

Continuing to walk through the thick desert, Trevis heard the horrific howl of the wind and the taste of salt and death filled his mouth.

An odd memory from the first time, he arrived in this Queen forsaken country of Mortisitical. All the new arrivals were ordered to spend a night in the desert.

Even as a new recruit, Trevis hated this place with a passion. The sand, the sounds, the snakes! He hated them all.

So, the thought of spending more time in this horrific place was outrageous and his nightmare.

Randomly he started to laugh at himself as he remembered his father's offer to get him to take over the family business.

Perhaps being the Queen's engineer would be better than walking through rough sand?

After a few moments more of him walking and with his feet sinking into the vile sand, Trevis stopped. The wind continued to rub away at his skin. Making his face warm from the pain.

Trevis started to look around to think what in the

Queen's name he was doing out in the middle of nowhere, unloved and exiled into solitude.

When the Ordoicous Army was attacked by the nation of Mortisical. It was meant to be a simple war to get revenge for past transgressions. Trevis started smiling. How long ago that all seemed but Tervis had committed transgressions himself. He bit his lip as the memories of the rage of his comrades came into his memory.

His heart started to beat a little faster at the thought that his friends would kill him for committing something they termed as treacherous. Then he remembered his only chance of living was a death oath.

Trevis continued to walk forwards. He was alone and that is how it had to be. He wanted to die alone, fighting for his Queen once more.

In the distance, Trevis heard the disgraceful sound of the enemy firing mortar shells and cannons. The thought disgusted him. He knew these foes were firing on their citizens and twisting the corpses to remind their people that the Ordoicous were the enemy.

The sound of metal came from behind Trevis.

He beamed.

A whispering came through the air.

Trevis jumped forward.

He turned around.

To see two men in black metal armour swing their long silver swords at him.

Trevis whipped out his own grey longsword.

He swung it.

The two men met it.

A great clang barely made it over the howling wind.

Both of the men unleashed a flurry of attacks.

Trevis beamed at the idea of his death.

He met and deflected the blows.

One of the enemies charged forward.

Trevis dived out the way.

The man fell forward.

Trevis rammed his blade through the man's chest.

The sand wasn't yellow anymore.

The other man punched Trevis in the head.

Trevis fell back a few metres.

The enemy sword smashed into his right wrist.

Trevis dropped his sword.

The last enemy charged at him.

Trevis stepped to one side. The man went past. Trevis grabbed the man's arm and pulled it behind his back.

A disgusting crush and snap managed to reach Trevis' ears as he snapped the man's arm. Before he snapped his neck.

Trevis looked to the other corpses that was almost buried by the sand. He walked over to the body and ripped off the smooth black cloth the man had tied around his face. Trevis did the same.

He almost regretted it as his nose was filled with the disgusting smell of sweat and blood. Yet Trevis didn't have much of a choice, not with the wind blowing as much as it did.

Kneeling on the ground, Trevis began to look through the armour of the man who almost killed him. But the cold metal armour was too tight to hide anything.

As Trevis was feeling the man's ankles, he felt something leading into the man's boot. Pulling it out he saw it was a wrecked parchment map of some sort.

The exiled soldier scratched his head as he attempted to make out of the cruelly drawn landscapes of the area. Which was almost impossible considering the constantly shifting nature of the desert with all the wind.

After a few seconds, he saw some strange triangle symbol labelled *Home*. Trevis took a deep breath. Knowing he had his objective and hopefully his chance to die for his Queen.

***

Despite the wind dropping to a mere whisper, the thick rough yellow sand still blew slowly in the warm air. Creating swirling masses of sand. The sand coated Trevis' throat in a thin layer of rough abrasive sand.

He kept wanting to cough but he was on a mission and he remembered the cost of even a simple cough can have on him and his mission.

Focusing on the desert ahead of him, Trevis' eyes narrowed and through the thick masses of swirling sand. A few metres from him, he saw his target. It might have been a few metres from him, but the swirling sand cloaked his position perfectly.

In addition, to the pitch-black night sky overhead. He knew he was safe. No enemy or no one sensible would be awake at this hour. Especially, with the endless number of predatory hunters stalking the desert for prey.

Thankfully, the three bright moons shone brightly through the swirling sand. Allowing Trevis to focus on his target before he striked.

Focusing in detail, Trevis studied the three white cone tepee tents made from thick animal hide metres away from one another. Outside each tent was a crackling roaring fire that deafened all other noises.

Trevis beamed a little at the thought of having a fertile killing ground with a fire to burn the tents, whilst the enemy slept, and to block out the screams of the enemy he killed.

Taking a final look, Trevis noticed a larger rectangular dirty white tent in the middle of the triangle of the other tents. With a small door flapping in the wind and spears laying on the sandy floor outside.

Trevis took out his long grey dagger that shone in the moonlight and stroked his thumb down its leathery rough handle. He had killed so many with his blades for the Queen, what were a few more lives?

All he desired in all the world was a chance to die. A chance to fulfil his duty to the Queen and end his endless cycle of loneliness.

Of course, Trevis had a loving brother and father back in Ordoicous. Yet that was a lifetime ago. His father was probably dead and his brother… disowned him.

A tear wanted to run down Trevis' face but he willed the tear to stay in his eye. It ran down his face anyway. He loved his brother but if that was true. Why couldn't he support his brother when he needed him the most?

Looking back at the dagger, Trevis held it tightly in his hand and slowly walked towards the camp. He would kill these foes of the Queen for Her and his family.

As he passed through the swirling masses of sand, the smell of burning wood and meat filled his senses.

Stepping towards one of the tepees, Trevis carefully touched the canvas edge, the cold material feeling good against his warm fingers. Pulling it open, he stepped inside.

The smell of sweaty men filled his nose and Trevis wanted to gag, but he needed to remain focused.

Despite the pitch black, his eyes quickly adjusted to see the outline of two sleeping faces lying on the ground only a few steps away.

Then one of them started snoring.

Trevis hated snoring.

His father used to snore terribly.

Trevis whipped out his blade.

Thrusting into the throat of the snoring man.

The tent was silent.

Quickly, Trevis whipped out the blade and split the throat of the other man.

Slowly, a strange sense of wonder and fear washed over him. Trevis started to sweat. These weren't his feelings, it almost felt as if someone was forcing their feelings into him.

Trevis dismissed the notion.

He took a few more steps into the tent and saw a final soldier sleeping.

Trevis stood there for a moment, looking at the man. He looked so peaceful, so loved. He could have had a family, a wife, a husband back home.

It did not matter. Trevis whipped out his dagger and forced it through the man's neck.

Again, a strange feeling of fear and desperation washed over him.

In case these were his own feelings. Trevis rubbed his forehead focused on the fact that these three dead soldiers were never going to hurt his Queen.

Again, a strange sensation washed over him but Trevis felt drawn to the tent in the middle of the camp. Trevis tried to resist but he wanted to look, he wanted to know what was inside.

Opening the door of the tepee, Trevis walked through swirling masses of sand and small columns of smoke over to the large tent. The smell of urine was unbearable, but he persisted. Trevis tried one last time to resist the idea of going inside but he could not.

He went inside.

Surprisingly enough, the tent was lit with rows upon rows of tiny candles hanging from the wooden joints in the 'ceiling' of the tent.

Illuminating the great piles of treasures around the tent. From the great pile of golden to Trevis' left to the pile of jewels to Trevis' right.

He took a few steps closer towards the immense desk made from solid oak wood, with gold highlighting the unique curves and knobs of the wood. In addition to the piles of parchment littered on the desk.

Yet what caught Trevis' eyes was the bronze cage in the middle of the desk with a small cat-like creature inside. With thick velvety fur in a wide range of dark purple, violet, and blue shades.

A part of Trevis stared in awe at the creature. The other part of him wanted to run from it.

The Cat Creature's eyes sparkled with magical

energy and Trevis felt a wave of awe wash over him.

He took a few steps away.

Then a wave of the familiar washed over him- loneliness. This cat creature was alone. This creature existed in solitude.

Hands grabbed Trevis from behind.

He struggled.

He kicked.

The enemy got Trevis into a headlock.

Another man bought forward a metal chair.

The enemy forced Trevis onto the chair.

Before knocking him out.

A wave of fear washed over him.

***

As his awareness returned, Trevis tried to move but he couldn't. He tried to turn his wrists but the rough rope that bound him dug in tighter.

Trevis could feel his skin-tight and ready to burst. Spilling all his blood onto the sand below him. Yet he couldn't do that either.

All this time he wanted to die for his Queen, but he knew this wasn't his time. He had something to do first.

Trying to move his feet, Trevis only felt his leather boots digging into the rough irritating sand more as a few grains of the horrible stuff entered his boots.

His vision cleared.

Trevis shot back in shock, well he tried.

In front of him were three heavily muscular men with thick Crimson red Knight armour with bronze icons of skulls, daggers and blood on their armour.

But on each of their shoulder pads was a golden eye crying bloody tears.

As he focused on that symbol, Trevis started to sweat and his heart raced.

That was the symbol of the Mortis Guard.

What were elite stormtroopers doing outside the capital or away from major war zones?

These were not the types of troopers you leave to their own devices. These are the people you call when you're planning something big.

Trevis tried to figure out their plan to no avail.

This was his purpose, he had to find out the reason and stop them.

Narrowing his eyes, Trevis stared at each of them but in their armour, they were all indistinguishable. With their jet black helmet and Ruby red eye pieces.

Although, Trevis clocked his head at the smell of sweetly perfumed oils in the air that these soldiers gave off. He had heard of naked oil rituals but this smelt strange and excessive. It was all he could smell.

The metal cage made a noise as the cat creature banged against its prison.

The three Knights wondered over to the cat on the desk and picked up the cage.

Trevis struggled in his bonds hoping to get free, but the ropes dug into his skin more.

A wave of appreciation washed over him.

One of the men reached behind his back and grabbed a small knife.

The cat focused on the blade.

Another man opened the cage door.

The blade kept closer to the door.

Trevis screamed.

He wasn't going to let the cat die.

The three men turned to him.

Allowing the cat to shoot out the cage.

A purple blur raced across the tent.

More irritating sand coated Trevis' skin.

Two of the men chased after it.

The purple blurb chased across the room again and again.

The two men struggled to chase it.

Jumping, leaping and diving for the cat.

Trevis smiled.

There was another purple blur and Trevis felt a claw catch his wrists.

The other Knight walked over to Trevis.

Whacking him across the face.

Trevis' face pulsed with pain.

A loud howl gave from the opposite side of the tent as the two men grabbed the cat.

Trevis' heart sank.

The cat howled a little more.

The man who whacked Trevis took a few steps closer to him. He could feel the man's body warmth and his awful smell strong and stinking at this distance.

In a heavy accent, the man uttered: "How did you know we were here?"

Trevis bit his lip.

A wave of support came from the cat.

"How did you know?" the man pressed.

Trevis stayed silent.

The man shook his head and got out his small knife. Pointing it at the cat.

"You were clearly abandoned. No one will come for you. You are alone,"

Trevis looked to the sandy ground.

"Ha. You have no information for me, So, unless you have something for me. I will kill you,"

The man came closer.

Trevis longed for this moment, but he looked at the cat. He didn't want this moment, not anymore.

The man came closer.

Trevis jumped up.

His frayed ropes breaking free.

Trevis knocked the man to the ground. Fighting for the knife.

The other men screamed as the cat bit them hard.

Loud screams and shouts from outside the tent filled the chamber.

The man with the knife was distracted.

Trevis kicked him in between the legs. Before grabbing the knife.

The cat howled.

Trevis rushed over to see the two men fighting with the cat.

He rapidly thrusted the knife into one of the man's back.

The screams outside got louder.

The cat jumped on the other man. Clawing his eyes out.

A wave of panic washed over Trevis.

A sword shot out of his chest. Before the final man ripped out the blade.

Trevis stumbled to the sandy floor. Staring with cold intent at the man with his sword dripping his blood.

The cat howled with murderous rage, but the man's head cracked like an egg as a gunshot went off.

Trevis' eyes widened as he saw multiple soldiers with their heavy yet flexible armour and their strange goggles over their eyes. But most importantly, the Ordoicous symbols on their shoulder pads marched in with their rifles aimed high. Scanning the rest of the chamber.

One of the soldiers gracefully marched to Trevis and ripped off the piece of cloth that he used to protect himself from the sand. The soldier stroked his face with care, but Trevis knew whose eyes were behind those goggles.

A solider who bought so much pain to his family and his kingdom but none of it was ultimately his fault.

"Daniel, take the cat and look after it. But stay away from my family,"

Trevis had no idea what Daniel said to him as the darkness claimed him. But a sense of regret filled him as he died.

He was wrong. He was never alone. His friends were always with him

HEART OF THE STANDING

The noise, the noise, the noise.

I really do hate the noise but I have to admit as I awkwardly stand outside this ugly shop window filled with flowers in every shape, size and colour imaginable. I must admit humans are funny creatures.

As I looked up and down the busy grey cobblestone rocks, seeing all the people going about their day whilst their disgusting sweaty smell fills the air, I'm definitely reminded why I don't like going out. I would much prefer to just stay in the Castle and tend to the great Fireheart family business of selling military supplies to the Queen.

I know lots of people think of me as weird for being so dedicated to my family business but I see it as me making a difference. By helping the Queen, I get to help others and make Ordericous a safer place. And that's all I want.

The noise of people chatting and shouting only made me more irritated for being out here. I know I probably think or say this a lot but I do love my autism but it does have its downsides.

A part of me wonders what a person without autism might feel now. Happiness to see all these noisy smelly people? Perhaps but I really don't care what other people think.

Putting those thoughts aside, I felt the hot afternoon sun beat down on my face and black leather trench coat. Feeling drops of sweats run down my back, I supposed I better get into some shade but I would happily suffer a little longer in this heat. Again, weird but everyone in my family is weird to some extent because of our magical gifts. Yet at least I could now understand why all these people were so smelly.

Although, it was only now I knew the worse part of smelling all these disgusting sweaty people was it left a foul salty taste in my mouth!

Now I really wanted to go.

But the entire reason I'm standing out here was because I'm waiting for my beautiful Harrison to come out. I knew he wanted to be nice to me by getting me some flowers. He said it would be romantic. But I really don't care about some flowers that will be dead in a few days. I love him. That's all that matters to me.

Well, that and I would love to get out of here and spend some proper time with him. I definitely wouldn't mind admiring his beautiful longish soft blond hair and that stunning face.

Then it dawned on me, he had been in there for quite a while. The only reason why I didn't go in there was because of all those flowers and extremely strong smells would annoy me too much. Yet I do question my logic of standing outside on a busy smelly street. Had something happened to him?

Taking a deep disgusting sweat filled breath, I played with my dulled blade in my hand slowly as I considered the problem.

The street was emptying.

It was hardly as if secret members of the Triad weren't hunting me and Harrison for being gay abominations. We still didn't know who these people, who wanted to kill the Queen, were. Could one of them have taken Harrison to get the Queen and my family?

The street kept emptying.

My dulled blade started to spin quicker in my hand.

I moved my free hand down to my sword hilt, its cold metal feeling refreshing against my skin, as I prepared. I couldn't let anything happen to Harrison.

The street was completely empty.

Then I finally realised, I was alone in a street that was jam packed only minutes ago. At least the street smelt better!

Without these noisy people around me I could actually see the grey cobblestone road clearly and all the various bright shops on the other side of the road. But where did everyone go?

A part of me was willing me to go and check on Harrison. After all he was one of the few people I had actually formed a bond with. I can't really afford to lose him. That and I did love him.

Turning around, feeling the smooth cobblestone under my feet, I walked over to the large wooden door to the shop and wrapped my hand tightly around the warm metal doorknob.

I tried to open it.

It wouldn't open.

I pulled it with both hands.

My knuckles white.

It still wouldn't open.

Multiple footsteps echoed around the road.

In case this was some kind of threat from some stupid people I slowly turned around. Allowing my feet to press hard into the cobblestone ground. My dulled blade spinning fast in my hand.

After I turned around the air smelt old and stale. Not surprising considering the five disgusting men that stood in front of me. Their clothes were basically foul rags and covered in thick black grease, as was their foul hair.

Everything about these men was disgusting even when they gave me a menacing smile it only showed the rotten stumps of their black teeth.

These men definitely didn't come from Fireheart land, we look after our people.

Men whipped out sharp shiny daggers with bright golden hilts.

These smelly people definitely didn't get them themselves. Much too high a quality for these people to afford.

I whipped out my massive sword. It's cold metal firmly in my hand.

"Ya Freak of a boyfriend fine for now," the man in the middle said in a voice that was an assault on my sensitive ears. I supposed he had to be the leader.

I wanted to rip his throat out there and then.

"We gonna gut him soon," another man said.

Whoever these people were I really wanted to kill them. I didn't have time for homophobes and haters not after everything I've been through.

At the thought, my arms ached as the memories of my self-inflicted cuts came back.

But despite all the hate and my past, I was still standing. Today would be no different.

"Looky here lads the Freak still isn't talking," the leader said.

"Let's cut that Freaky face up and do our mission," another man said.

Now, I had to smile at these stupid fools. As much as I don't like people talking I will always admit sometimes you need to let them chat on.

At least now I knew these haters were working for the Triad.

A part of me hoped these hired blades could help us with our investigation. But another part of me just wanted to slaughter them.

"Watch out boys the Freak's smiling. He might like us," the leader said.

"Let's kill the Freak!" The others shouted.

I really needed to check on Harrison.

Was he okay?

Was he hurt?

The men charged at me.

Their blades shone in the sunlight.

I whacked one of the men.

He fell back.

Smashing his head onto the floor.

Blood poured out.

Somehow he got back up.

He smiled.

They all charged at me with their daggers.

I whipped out my sword. Slashing and lashing at them.

They darted back.

Then ran at me.

Daggers flashed as they moved rapidly.

I jumped back.

Hitting the warm glass of the shop window.

The men thrusted out their blades.

I dropped to the floor.

Their daggers chipped the glass.

I jumped up. Smashing my fists into the jaws of two men.

They collapsed to the ground.

The other men paused.

I did not.

I grabbed one of them.

Smashing my fists into his head.

He collapsed to the floor.

I slammed my foot back on his head.

Blood and brain matter exploded out.

The air became thick with fearful sweat.

One dead. Four to go.

A sharp right hook knocked me back.

How dare he touch me!

I hate being touched!

Lashing my sword wildly. I slashed the throat of one man.

Blood gushed out of the wound.

I kicked the body to the ground.

The Leader flew at me.

Twirling and swirling his dagger at me.

I rapidly dodged each blow.

He was quick.

The other men joined in.

Tens of wild jabs came at me.

I was quick.

Not quick enough.

One dagger sliced my arm.

My entire arm flooded with pain from my older wounds.

I screamed.

Another man kicked me in the head.

My sword went flying.

My face slammed into the shop's window.

My blood smeared over the glass.

Rage built inside me.

These men grabbed my long hair. Pulling it painfully.

They ripped my hair back. Revealing my throat.

"You gonna die now Freak. You Freaks are disgusting. Men on men… is just wrong," the foul leader said.

I stared into his cold stupid eyes.

"Don't ya worry. We're gonna kill your freak of a man later," said another man.

My dulled blade rapidly turned in my hand.

I couldn't let anything happen to Harrison.

Rage continued to build inside me.

Two powerful memories came into my mind. Two very simple solutions. Two times I saved the day.

The men bought their daggers to my throat.

They tensed.

I had had enough.

I unleash my power.

My eyes glazed over.

My skin became hard and rough.

I dropped my Dulled Blade.

My long nails hardened into razor sharp talons.

My teeth turned to fangs.

The men tried to split my throat.

It didn't work.

My skin was too thick.

Their eyes widened.

Sweat dripped down their faces.

I smiled.

Whacking them with my talons, I smiled and jumped up.

I charged over to them.

Ripping their flesh apart.

Sinking my fangs into their juicy rich flesh.

They screamed in agony.

Screaming to some member of the Triad that had abandoned them.

My fangs devoured their delicious flesh.

Their bones crushed and snapped.

I finished off two men easily.

I span around.

Charging over to another man, I crushed his legs with my immense feet. My talons sinking into his stomach.

I slashed his stomach open.

His guts and stomach rushed out.

I scooped them up. Downing them in one.

Before I whacked his head clear off.

Turning around slowly I saw the leader had managed to crawl over to me. His dagger pointed straight at me.

I had to laugh at the pointlessness of it. As much as I hated to use my Flesheater ability, which is what this transformation is called, I was happy to use it to kill these haters. There was no place in the world for people like this.

I snarled at him. My fangs shining in his eyes.

He dropped the dagger.

Thrusting my claws into his chest, I picked him up.

"You see little Hater. You and your Triad will never win. Me, my family, the Queen and my so-called Freak of a boyfriend will survive,"

It looked as if he wanted to speak but I moved my claws inside him. He fought to bit down the pain. Silly mortal.

"Your Master or whoever paid you was stupid. They wanted you and your friends to die. Your Master would know after everything I have been through. I'm still standing. I'm alive. And that will not change because of stupid mortals like you,"

The Leader's eyes widened. Maybe in realisation or maybe in fear. I didn't care.

I smashed his pointless body into the ground.

My talon dripping with his rich red blood.

Knowing it was thankfully over, I needed to stop this weird ability. I forced myself to look around for my dulled blade.

Seeing it a few metres away, near the glass shop window with my smeared blood starting to dry, I wandered over to it and picked it up.

Taking long deep breaths, I focused on the feeling of the warm smooth metal in my hand and the stunning Harrison. His beautiful body and that wonderful longish blond hair. I just wanted him to be safe.

After a few moments, my teeth, skin and nails returned to normal. But I just wanted Harrison to be safe.

Walking over to the smooth metal doorknob, I

pulled and twisted it again. It still didn't move.

I had to break it down.

I need to make sure he's okay.

Taking a few steps back, I went to charge.

Then the door opened and my beautiful Harrison walked out in his stunning tight white tunic that highlighted his muscles. His beautiful hair parted to the left and lightly blowing in the wind that blew down the road.

Then to my horror in his hands were a… horrific brunch of red, pink and blue flowers with massive diamond shaped petals and thick oval leaves.

I had no idea what flowers they were but they stunk of intense sweet oranges and cinnamon.

But for some reason, I really didn't mind the flowers. My only concern and thought was my beautiful Harrison was okay. He was alive and unharmed. That's all that mattered.

Then Harrison looked around, focused on the slaughtered corpses and cocked his head at me.

I didn't want to explain anything. I loved him. I protected him that's all he needed to know. But most of all, I'm still standing.

HEART OF THE FLESHEATER

Cetus' eyes rapidly blinked as it attempted to readjust to the light.

After a few moments of constant blinking, his eyes opened. Cetus looked straight up. His eyes narrowing at the strange sight of the solid grey rock ceiling. It looked well aged and rough. Nothing pleasant in the slightest.

The unpleasantness was only added to by the odd smell of burning sage and onion that filled the air. But at least it made the taste of delicious stuffing form in his mouth.

He tried to move but immense pain tore at his wrists and ankles. Cetus paused trying to lift his head up to look at his ankles. He couldn't see them but his eyes widened as he saw the rough damaged bricks that made up the small room he was in. Where was he?

It looked like he was in some kind of chamber in the deepest darkest depths of a castle. But he had no idea why he was here?

He tried to remember what happened before he woke up. Nothing. Except he had a feeling that he had a family. Maybe a wife and two children but he couldn't picture them.

Pulling at his wrists again, pain pulsed violently down his arms. Turning his head to look at them, Cetus saw his wrists were tightly bound with thick yellow rope made from plants he didn't recognise.

Then it hit him. He was tied down as he felt his back ached against the hard cold white marble beneath him. His entire body ached from being tied up. Cetus didn't know how long he had been here. An hour? A day? A week? His joints were hurting so much he couldn't tell.

Although, after a few moments of thinking about that he felt like he 'remembered' something. A memory didn't form in his mind but he knew he was taken by a group. No he wasn't taken, he went willingly.

Cetus rested his head back down on the white marble, he didn't know what was going on. Why would he go with these people? And why couldn't he remember?

He pulled hard on the rope.

It dug into his flesh.

He snarled in pain.

Cetus paused. He snarled? He wasn't some crazy wolf or other monster. Cetus was a human. How could he snarl?

A part of Cetus wanted to... he didn't know. Cetus was trapped, alone and abandoned in this little castle chamber. He had no idea why he was here but he could suddenly snarl like some monster. And he really had a craving for flesh.

This was getting ridiculous. Cetus now wanted flesh. What was wrong with him. He just knew this wasn't normal.

The sound of an immense metal door shrieking open made Cetus pause. A set of light footsteps entered the little chamber whilst someone else shut and locked the door after her.

He tried to stretch his neck to see the person but it was useless. It was only a minute or two later when the figure, a woman, stepped into view.

Cetus dropped his mouth in amazement. This woman was beautiful. Her long life filled black hair floated in the air angelically. Her stunning smooth youthful face was a pure delight. Even this woman's violet eyes were a marvel to love. She was stunning. Cetus focused on those beautiful eyes as she smiled at him. And brushed some dirt off her pure white silky dress.

She gave him a seductive smile. "I am Primus Fateweaver. Do you know who you are?"

Cetus just focused on her beautiful words. They were so perfect, so velvety. They were like a siren's voice. He wanted to follow those words. He needed those words. Then he remembered the question.

But he couldn't. He couldn't remember his own name. Cetus got a sense that he had one and he loved his name. Why couldn't he remember it?

"I am not surprised you do not remember it. I am rather surprised you are alive after the experiment,"

Cetus tried to frown or question that statement in his mind but he couldn't. All he could focus on were those beautiful words from this stunning woman. Yet another part of him just wanted to taste some flesh and drink some nice warm blood.

He licked his lips.

"Interesting. Are you hungry?" the woman asked.

"Do you have some flesh?" Cetus asked. His eyes widening as he realised what he asked.

The woman smiled. "Of course, do you want something to drink?"

"Blood please. I need some blood," Cetus said.

The smallest part of his mind wanted to scream out. Telling him to stop and question what was happening. He couldn't remember anything but he knew this wasn't normal.

"I know your mind wants to question me. Do not let it. I am Primus Fateweaver. Do you know me?"

Cetus thought about the words. Then he noticed the woman had grabbed a large ruby covered dagger and sliced one of his arms free from the ropes. She gave him the knife.

Cetus didn't hesitate in continuing to cut himself free as she spoke.

"Primus Fateweaver. I am known to you humans. I am one but I am not. Do you know me?"

Cetus tried to cut himself free. "Fateweaver. Impossible. You're a children's story. I've read those stories before. Something about a witch who can spin the fate of people into what she desires,"

"Correct, I suppose. I am a witch of some kind. I can see the threads of fate. I can weave them to my desire. A kill there. A plague here. A forest fire over there. I manipulate events to my Endgame,"

Cetus cut his other arm free.

He forced himself up. His back aching after being tied down for so long, but how did he know he had read the stories before?

"Why am I here?" Cetus asked.

"Because I Willed it. You are a part of Fate. You are vital to my Endgame. You should feel honoured, humbled even,"

Cetus could feel something inside him grow. He knew he didn't want to be here. He wanted to escape. Yet Cetus really, really wanted to taste some flesh.

"Are you hungry yet?"

Cetus wanted to nod so badly. He forced his head to stay still.

"Why am I here?" Cetus asked. He cut one of his legs free.

"I wanted to experiment with you. I was successful. You are human no more. You are the next generation of us. You are a Flesheater,"

That name. Those words.

For the first time, Cetus paused as a strange memory came into his mind. He was tied down in this chamber but there were five cloaked people with him. Chanting. Screaming. They were carving him up. Adding strange potions. Then the word: Flesheater screamed into his mind.

He felt his nails starting to harden.

Cetus looked at Fateweaver.

"You should be honoured. I made you into something useful. You will be very helpful to me," Fateweaver said.

"I will not help you. I didn't want this,"

"How do you know?"

"Because…"

She was right. Cetus didn't know. He didn't know anything.

He cut his last foot free but when he looked at his nails. He was horrified. Cetus's nails were now long and twisted into bright yellow claws. Perfect for ripping out delicious, sweet flesh.

He licked his lips.

The woman came over to him. Taking the knife.

She sliced into her hand.

Beautiful dark red rich blood gushed out. Cetus knew it was beautiful. He wanted to drink some. He needed to drink some of that beautiful liquid.

Fateweaver wiped her other hand over the deep slice. Healing it instantly. Cetus's mood dropped. Disappointment filled him.

When the disappointment cleared, all Cetus could smell was the disgusting scent of mortal humans. These people were disgusting. Their sweat…

Then Cetus realised there was no one in here. He looked around for the woman but she was gone.

Standing up he forced himself to take a few steps forward. The movement felt strange and unnatural to him. Cetus looked down at his feet. Only to see immense talons instead of toes.

A part of him wanted to know what was happening to him. Then a memory of some people came into his mind. There was a woman, Fateweaver, talking to him. Showing him some ancient maps. She gave him some coin that he gave to his wife before leaving them.

Cetus sat back on the marble. The cold stone pulsing through him and breathing in the faint smell of long gone humans that left his mouth fantasying about their delicious flesh.

He tried to think about this problem. Cetus knew he was trapped and turning into something. He must have done this willingly may be to help or save his family. Yes, that sounded right.

The sound of the door creeping open made Cetus turn and stand.

A young woman was pushed hard into the chamber. Cetus had no idea how old she was. Maybe twenty. He had to admit she was attractive with her slim figure and long golden hair that flowed like an ocean down her long black dress. Should he help her? Talk to her?

Cetus took a step forward but then he saw a little cut on her forehead. A wave of sadness washed over him. Until he saw a drop of beautiful blood drip down her face.

He licked his lips.

Cetus didn't know why. He just wanted a little taste.

He tried to fight it.

Cetus wanted to resist.

He was hungry.

So hungry.

Cetus snarled.

Charging at her.

He felt his teeth grow into razor sharp fangs.

His claws growing in length and sharpness.

They shone in the light.

The young woman screamed in terror.

Cetus slashed her chest.

She screamed in agony.

He didn't care.

Her warm blood splashed up his chest.

Cetus laughed in utter delight.

He sunk his massive fangs into her flesh.

It was delicious. So sweet. So juicy. So…

***

When his vision tried to clear, Cetus could only

see blurs of shapes. Cetus tried to focus on his surroundings, but he couldn't. All he could smell was the delicious, if not disturbing, blood that must have covered the room along with piles of rotting flesh. He knew this was wrong but there was something good about it. Something he longed for. It left a sweet taste like juicy pork or barbecue ribs in his mouth.

Although, Cetus felt something hard and solid under him that pulsed warmth into his body. It wasn't unpleasant but he wanted it to stop.

Cetus tried to stand up, but pain flooded his wrists and ankles. It felt as if something was stabbing his joints. The harder he tried to move the worse the pain got.

After a moment or two, his vision cleared and he wanted to shoot back. But the solid thing (rock?) he was tied to stopped that. He looked at the five cloaked figures in their dark black cloaks and veils. Leaving no skin untouched but their chests showed they were all women.

Cetus hadn't heard it before but they were screaming at him. Chanting you might call it. He didn't know the language. It sounded strange and alien. Maybe Mortisical. Those people were strange in the far north.

The words were rough and violent. Like these women were screaming for help or screaming for demons to come.

Sweat dripped off his back and forehead. He really didn't want to be here.

Immense pain filled Cetus's body. He screamed out as his body flooded with agony. Almost like people were ripping his flesh out.

A strange sense of familiarity washed over him. It was like he had done this before. Not once, not twice. Maybe a thousand or tens of thousands of times.

A beautiful, angelic, velvety voice spoke into his mind.

"You have passed. I am Primus Fateweaver. Your new hope. Your Mother. I created you. You will help me with my Endgame. You shall weave the fates to my tune. All of the 9 Kingdoms shall bend their knee to me,"

Cetus just nodded in agreement against the screams of agony as he saw the women stab and slash his skin. Taking out organs and putting in potions and strange objects into him.

"You are my Flesheater. The First of your kin. You will be my sword but there is something so important you must do first. Will you do it?"

"Yes!" Cetus shouted.

All he wanted to do was serve this beautiful voice. He belonged to Fateweaver. He would serve her. No matter how dark the plot. Cetus just wanted to please her.

A small part of him shook his head briefly. This was wrong. He was no slave. He was free but as this tiny part of him made him shake his head. The voice spoke to him. Almost as if it was talking to this little part of him that was surviving this ritual.

"Your mind belongs to me. I am The Weaver of Fate. I will make sure you will never free him. I will make you watch as you kill men, women and children for me. Do you understand?"

For some reason, Cetus nodded his head. He didn't know why. He was happy to serve her. He wanted to kill for her. Cetus wanted to unleash his talons onto the flesh of mortals. He loved the feeling of their flesh.

"Cetus, I need you to mate with six people. There will be a Noble Family in a thousand years' time. I need one of them to be a Flesheater. Go now. Mate with six people then return to me. I must stop the House of Fireheart before they stop me in a thousand years,"

When Cetus heard those words, he blinked hard. Then he cocked his head as he didn't see any of the five women anymore. His body didn't hurt. He was fine, perfect even.

All he wanted to do was taste the flesh of mortals and drink their beautiful blood. But first he knew he had a mission. He needed to meet six people for some entertainment.

Standing up he found it weird the ropes were gone. But looking at the small door to the entrance of the little castle chamber, he saw it was wide open.

Cetus didn't waste any time. He walked out as fast as he could. Ready to complete his mission for the Weaver of Fate.

HEART OF A KILLER

It was happening all over again.

Hellen knew that as soon as she walked inside the damp mould covered wooden house with its small box like rooms. Hellen knew exactly where everything was here. From the little kitchen with a broken constantly dripping tap in the back to this main room that served as a living, dining and bedroom.

She frowned a little as she stepped over a mouldy broken plate in the doorway and she went inside further.

Her massive wooden stick tapped gently against the floor that crumbled with each step she took. Kicking up all sort of nasty things into the air.

Hellen took a few more steps as she stood on something that made her foot slimy and wet.

Inspecting the little house, a memory of her playing in here as a child with some of her friends sprang to mind. It was a lot nicer back then and this was a house that wasn't reduced to ruin. How times change.

The sound of the constantly dripping tap still went on in the background as Hellen remembered how disgusting that water tasted all those decades ago.

As she walked to the middle of the little house, she crushed a little toy covered in some sort of dead animal. A rat perhaps? Hellen really didn't want to find out.

The reason was she was here dressed in her grey Procurator coat was because she was an Officer of the Law working for the Queen and someone had randomly decided to end someone. Well that was what the report said.

Yet Hellen didn't remember too many of the details whilst her mind was still a little foggy after last night's... fun with one of the Royal Guards. Those people can move!

The sound of damp mould drew Hellen's focus back to the ruined house. The black mould covered every inch of this disgusting place. Hellen didn't know why the house was still standing. Everyone in Ordericous knew this was a health hazard in an unloved part of the country. Maybe she should throw her weight around and get it destroyed. It might stop a few people from getting sick. Maybe she would.

Turning around Hellen held her grey Procurator cloak over her nose as the air stunk of rotten meat and the sound of the flies buzzing reached her ears.

Looking over at the little dead yellow straw bed in the far corner of the little disgusting room, Hellen found exactly what she thought she would find. A half devoured corpse.

Simply lying there, stretched out on the straw bed for the rats and other foul creatures of the night to devour.

Hellen shook her head.

It was happening all over again.

Stepping carefully over to the corpse and bed, Hellen gagged as the smell of rotten flesh grew stronger and stronger. But thankfully the buzzing of the flies died down. Almost as if Hellen was scaring them.

After all, she had been told on more than one occasion of her scariness.

Standing only a metre away from the corpse, Hellen skilfully used her massive wooden stick to pull the flies and their lava off the victim.

Then Hellen had to frown and a wave of... sadness (she supposed) washed over her. She had seen this all before as she noted the flayed skin on the lower parts of the devoured body. Chunks of his skin still laid there attached to his body.

Moving her eyes up his body, Hellen supposed he must have been a strong lad once. Judging by a couple chunks of strong well defined abs that were barely eaten.

Then the real horror revealed itself. Judging by the saw and dagger marks on his chest, Hellen gave a deep frown as she thought about how the killer had carved out the man's still beating heart. Before making the victim watch his own heart beat whilst the foul killer continued to carve out their organs.

Hellen had to look away from the body.

Her studies at the Procurator academy only went so far. The real reason she sadly knew most of this was because she had seen the killer at work once. So long ago but not long enough.

Hellen walked over to the other side of the room. Listening to the dripping tap in the background and feeling the ruined floor under her feet.

The memory of investigating this killer, eventually finding him and then almost becoming his next victim flashed through her mind.

It was the same killer.

The memories of seeing the poor woman being killed in this horrific way always played in her mind at night. Having plenty of... special exercise helped but it never stopped the memories for long.

Looking over back at the corpse, Hellen made herself take a deep vile breath of this truly horrific damp mouldy air as she focused on this crime.

She might have failed to catch the killer once but not again. She was not going to let him take another life and that was a promise.

***

As Hellen breathed in the thick black smoke around her that left a foul bitter taste in her mouth, she frowned at the immense metal cladded warehouses that stretched back for as far as the eye could see and tens of metres into the sky. Housing all sorts of carriages, workshops and tools needed for repairing ships. Their metal cladding was an assault on the eyes with its ugly grey and rusted look.

Hellen lent against one of the metal cladded warehouses, its cold metal sending chills through her soft Procurator cloak, and she looked around with a frown at this square of open ground surrounded by these warehouses.

She dug the end of her massive wooden stick in the gravel covered ground. Listening to the gravel moan a little amongst the sounds of ships and dockworkers a few hundred metres away. Then the faint sound of waves hitting the edge of the docks tens of metres away reminded Hellen of how unloved this part of the docks were.

Casting her mind back, she remembered her father mentioning how busy and crazy the docks were every day. With thousands of ships coming into the harbour AND docks carrying everything you could imagine. Then her father would comment on how strange it was that you could never hear the waves because of the shouting of orders and everything else.

She smiled as she remembered her father. A lot of people she worked for shunned her for coming from a family of dockers. The lowest of the low. Commoners to the core. But Hellen just wanted to whack these people with her stick. She was a proud docker. Her father always said being a docker was the best job.

Hellen didn't know if she agreed with him on that but being a docker wasn't a bad job. It kept her family alive and well.

A loud crash of a wave in the distance made Hellen focus back on the ugly warehouses. The killer had to be here. This was where he lived. At least when she had tracked him down the first time, and this was his only option for a hideout.

From the eccentric (to put it nicely) Lady Serpentine running the underground caves to the Queen redeveloping all unused land. This was the only place left where no one would come looking.

Hellen had to smile at herself then. She had worked it all out and tracked the killer where all those posh annoying snobs couldn't. Sometimes Hellen really wanted to whack them with her stick to shut them up. Then she reminded herself she needed to find him first.

A small deep laugh echoed around the little circle of warehouses.

Hellen picked up her massive stick. Ready to whack something.

Something fell from the sky.

Hellen jumped.

Something splashed against the hard gravel.

Blood spattered up her legs.

Hellen looked at the thing in front of her. It was a heart. A cleanly sliced out heart.

Touching it briefly, Hellen could still feel the warmth pulse through it. This heart was a fresh kill.

Something landed on Hellen.

Knocking her to the ground.

Hellen's face smashed into the gravel.

Slicing her head.

Pushing herself back up, she knew exactly what it was as she pushed the thing off her.

It was a corpse.

A fresh warm corpse. The fresh still-vibrant rich red blood dripped out of the many wounds. It was impossible to tell if this person was a man or woman. There were simply too many cuts and injuries. From the warm pieces of flayed skin from the legs that flapped in the gentle breeze to where all the organs had been carefully carved out from the still living victim.

A part of Hellen wanted to whack herself with her massive stick. She was a failure. Her arrogance of thinking she was so smart to know where the killer was had made her lazy. She knew the killer was here. But instead of hunting this part of the docks high and low. Hellen simply stood there waiting for the killer to come to her.

The posh snobs wouldn't have waited. They would have searched the place. They- Hellen cut herself off. She knew thinking wasn't helpful. After all she was a Procurator, a good one. And if all that failed to make her feel good then at least she could say to people she was a best friend with the daughter of a Noble Family who was a Dominicus Procurator herself. That always made people silent and run away at parties.

Hellen bit her lip she was right about the killer being here. But she also knew the next part. Just like before, the Killer revealed his location to Hellen then the horror of this man was revealed.

Hellen's hand tightened around her massive stick making her knuckles turn white. Because unlike last time, she would stop this killer or she would die trying. Hellen couldn't go back to her Dominicus Procurator a failure.

***

After an hour of trying to find a way to the roof, Hellen had finally made it. She couldn't believe how hard it was to find a ladder. It was ridiculous. She didn't even want to think about how dock workers use to get up here for their extra… activities.

As she stepped off the ladder onto the cold hard metal rooftop, she gasped. This was beautiful. For tens upon tens of metres either side of her was nothing except dirty hard metal roofing. But the impressive part was the view.

Up here Hellen could see almost all of Ordericous, the beautiful busy harbour with tens of ships docking and unloading, the stunning castle and city in the distance and the lush forests behind her. This was beautiful. Perhaps she could bring a boy here one day for some fun.

The smell of sweat and salt reminded her of her father after a hard day's work at the dock. Then the sound of someone hitting metal made her look to her right.

In the distance, there was a black humanoid shape near the edge, presumably close to where she was standing below earlier.

Sweat dripped down her back and forehead. All her skin turned cold and numb. Her knuckles went white gripping her massive stick. She wanted to whack something.

Walking towards the black humanoid shape, Hellen had to fight herself to keep her mind focused. What if the Killer took her?

What if the Killer attacked her?

What if-

Hellen focused herself to stop. It was all useless. If her best friend Alessandria Fireheart had taught her anything, it was the importance of staying calm. As much as Hellen just wanted to whack people over the head, Alessandria might have a point in this case.

To force her mind off the Killer, Hellen focused on the hard metal roofing that banged and creeped with every step.

There was a shard of rusty metal on the ground.

Not sure if the Killer was watching her, she grabbed it. Sliding it into her pocket.

The smell of sweat and salt from earlier become faint. Being replaced with her own fear and the smell of rotten meat.

As she got closer to the black humanoid shape, Hellen could start to make out it was a man dressed in black leather. Holding something long and silver dripping dark red liquid.

She needed to be prepared but Hellen wanted to run.

She wanted to run away and never see this man.

Hellen remembered the horrors of seeing this man kill before. Her own fear back then had stopped her from arresting this deranged Killer. She was not going to let that happen again.

When Hellen was only a few metres away from him, she stopped. This Killer was disgusting. The black leather was no normal leather. It was human leather. Made from the freshly flayed skin of his victims. It lovingly hugged his strong muscular frame.

As she suspected this foul Killer was holding a long sharp sword dripping blood in one hand. But in the other hand, he was holding a strange dagger that glowed bright red at her. The closer she got, the brighter it glowed.

Forcing herself to down her fear, Hellen looked at him in the eye, those massive crazy white eyes that beamed at her. Maybe he liked her flesh. He definitely wasn't the first man, but he wasn't her type.

More sweat dripped down her back.

Hellen sighed. "By the Power of the Procuratorus, I am placing ya under arrest," she said.

The man cocked his head.

Did he not understand the words?

A weight pressed against Hellen's chest. She didn't know what to do now. Should she try and arrest him?

Slowly, Hellen started to walk over to the man. Trying to make sure she didn't make any sudden moves.

He coughed.

Hellen almost jumped but she didn't want to look weak.

Those massive crazy white eyes followed Hellen as she walked.

The bright red dagger glowed even brighter. It looked red hot.

It *was* red hot. Smoke started to pour from the foul man's hand.

He screamed.

Charging at Hellen.

She thrusted out her massive stick.

He dodged.

He slashed his sword at her.

She raised her massive stick. Before whacking him with it.

His jaw cracked briefly.

The red dagger flashed.

A magical wave of energy threw Hellen to the ground.

Her face smashed into the rusty metal roofing.

The man jumped into the air.
Hellen whacked him again.
He went flying.
He landed with a thud. Denting the roof.
Those massive crazy eyes opened even wider.
The dagger started glowing again.
Screaming the man charged at Hellen.
His sword swirled and twirled rapidly in the air.

Hellen tried to dodge all the attacks.
He was too quick.
He sliced her hand deep.
Dark red blood poured out.
The Killer screamed in utter delight.
Hellen went to cover her hand.
He slashed at her again.
Hellen tried to block.
The Killer grabbed her massive stick. Pulling hard.

Pain flooded Hellen's sliced hand.
She released.
The man punched her.
Her other hand let go.
The Killer threw her massive stick off the roof.

Hellen's body filled with rage.
How dare he.
She charged at him.
Punching and kicking.
The Killer was quick.
Perfectly dodging each attack.
The dagger glowed red hot once again.
A magical wave threw Hellen to the edge of the roof.

Hellen saw the ground tens of metres below.
She tried to keep her balance.
The man pushed her over.
Hellen grabbed onto the edge of the roof.
Her fingers hating the feel of the cold sharp metal.
Her knuckles ghostly white as she clung to the edge.
Her mind raced.
Was she going to die?
Would she fall?

After a few moments, the disgusting Killer stepped over the edge of the warehouse. Only a few centimetres away from Hellen's hands. Looking out over Ordericous. Almost admiring the view. The arrogant little so and so.

Hellen wanted to grab those foul human leather legs and pull him over the edge. But she knew she wasn't strong enough. He needed to be weakened first.

Those massive crazy white eyes looked down on her. Hellen wanted to rip them out.

He smiled. "Ya that one. The one tried to stop me. The Procurator that hide when I played with that person. Ya could have come out to play. I love a play mate. That blood and meat was delicious. Ya should have tried some,"

A part of Hellen wanted to let go. She didn't want to listen to this. But she had her duty to do.

"You will never win. If ya kill me-"

"I don't want to kill ya. I want a play mate. I want to have fun with ya. If not, I'll get ya body and chop ya up,"

Those crazy eyes almost lit up at the thought.

Hellen's heart raced.

"Won't that spoil my flavour?"

The Killer paused for a moment. Looking up at the sky.

She needed to think.

"Na," the man said.

He raised his foot to stamp on her hands.

Hellen didn't want to die.

She whipped out the rusty metal shard.

She thrusted it into the man's other leg.

He screamed.

Those crazy white eyes shutting in pain.

He started to fall towards the edge.

Hellen grabbed him. Throwing him off the roof.

The sound of smashing bones and spattering blood echoed behind her.

***

Looking at the pile of smashed up flesh, bones and brain matter in front of her, Hellen couldn't help but smile.

As she felt the rough gravel beneath her booted feet and heard the shouting of men in the distance with the gentle crashing of the waves too. Hellen knew she had completed her duty and completed her mission. That's all she ever wanted. Well that and some special fun.

Looking over at the warehouses around her with their ugly metal cladding, she knew this place was condemned and soon would be redeveloped by the Queen. Maybe that was a good thing. It might help erase this monster's legacy.

With her massive stick that she found closer

to the pile of flesh, Hellen whacked the human leather for no particular reason. Except now she could say she had successfully whacked him more than once or twice. And in her experience, it was always good to make sure the criminal was dead.

Breathing in the salty air from the nearby sea made Hellen pause. Her work today was of course small in the grand scheme of things, but she had made a difference. At least this would never happen again.

HEART OF ARMS

Alessandria knew she couldn't refuse her oldest friend's request to meet, but considering she was meeting the Queen. Alessandria would have thought the meeting place to be more welcoming.

Walking into the meeting place the roar and crackle of the bright yellow and orange fire filled the air. As it burnt in an ancient fireplace on the back wall. The smell and taste of charred wood and smoke filled her senses. Around the fireplace, the bricks were old and damaged. They were easily a century old.

Alessandria took a few more steps, feeling the warmth of the fire despite it being metres away. A drop of sweat dripped down her back.

Turning her head slightly, Alessandria frowned at this dirty, disgusting place in the castle. It was horrid. So many dusty, musty books on half destroyed shelves lined the entire room.

Maybe this was once an office, a library or something else entirely. It was impossible to tell.

All that Alessandria knew was she wouldn't choose to come back here. And if she did she would bring a maid to clear it first. The perks of being a Noblewoman.

The sound of someone shuffling playing cards made Alessandria turn to the left to see a very familiar face.

Sitting perfectly straight in a stunning angelic white dress, the Queen sat waiting for Alessandria. Her youthful features smooth and soft, and men would almost certainly call her stunning. But she knew that the Queen had a bit. Alessandria had seen that before!

Although, she had to admit the table and chair the Queen sat on were… questionable at best.

The table was utterly foul with its large rough circular top and woodworm infested legs. This table was useless. Just to prove a point to the Queen, Alessandria pressed a finger into the table. It cracked. The rotten wood turning into some kind of powder. Alessandria wiped her hand clean.

Thankfully, there was another chair next to the Queen so Alessandria sadly sat down. The cold smooth wood feeling fragile against her fingers as she carefully pulled in her chair.

She didn't want to. She didn't even want to be here. The only thing Alessandria wanted was to be with her friend. But the Queen had summoned her here for a reason. And Alessandria needed to find out what.

Again the Queen shuffled the decks of cards. Alessandria wanted to comment on the cards since the Queen never shuffled them. Alessandria knew the excuse was the Queen didn't want to break her nails. Why was she shuffling now?

As much as Alessandria had wanted to spend the night with her beautiful boyfriend Nemesio. This definitely had a hint of mystery to it.

Equally Alessandria would love to do some research in the Grand Library to try and find out more about the Triad. Some silly Masterminds who were trying to kill the Queen. But still this had some intrigue to it.

Alessandria nodded to her Queen. "You didn't invite me here to play cards did you like the good old days?"

"Dearest Lady Fireheart, you know your Queen too well and I must apologise for any deception used tonight," the Queen said.

As soon as the Queen had called her by her formal title, Alessandria wanted to tense and prepare for battle. The sound of her formal title coming from her Queen made her feel strange and uncomfortable.

Instead Alessandria looked around to see if anyone was here. There wasn't. Just shelves upon shelves of musty books.

"Your Majesty, why are you being formal? There is no one here. Just you and me,"

The Queen was silent.

Then Alessandria remembered something her brother Daniel had told her about his last meeting with the Queen.

"You bought me here on official business, *your Majesty*. Daniel said you were formal to him when you talked shop,"

"Your Brother is right, Lady Fireheart and I have bought you here for an official job," the Queen said.

It was just typical Alessandria had left her sword back in her bed chamber. That's the last time she listens to her boyfriend about carrying a sword in the safe castle.

"Whatever you need," Alessandria said.

The Queen nodded and gestured towards something on the wall.

Turning her head, Alessandria almost missed the dirty metal coat of arms under all the cobwebs.

Alessandria cocked her head as she looked at the stunning array of dirty colours. The coat of arms was a massive rectangular shield with a snake and two other lines dividing the shield into four quarters.

Each quarter had a striking design that made Alessandria puzzled. She recognised two of the patterns from textbooks. The top left quarter was of a type of triangular mosaic made of fiery red and yellows. Forming some kind of triangular pattern but the cobwebs made it difficult to see.

But the other quarter Alessandria recognised was a lot more beautiful. The top right quarter was a stunning blue wavey pattern like a tidal design.

Turning back to the Queen, Alessandria wanted to shrug. Why was this any of her concern? She had learnt about the coat of arms at school and in her various history lessons. But the coat of arms was hardly an excuse to see her.

"Do you know what each of these quarters represents?" the Queen asked.

A part of Alessandria wanted to be posh and all-knowing, but she was hardly that sort of Noble. Nor did she want to be associated with them in the slightest.

"Only the top two quarters, and isn't that snake meant to be the Snake of Betrayal? Something about a former King who betrayed the people and Nobility,"

The Queen nodded. "Correct, Lady Fireheart. The Snake is how my family got to become the Royal Family. Over 700 years ago, my family transitioned from a Noble Family to a Royal Family,"

For some reason that was genuinely interesting. It still didn't explain why Alessandria was here?

"Before you grow too desperate to learn why you are here, Lady Fireheart. I will explain that each quarter represents an Order of my Inquisition,"

Just hearing the name of that organisation made Alessandria want to tense. The memories of those horrible people and everything they had done to her, and her family flooded into her mind.

Taking a calming deep breath, Alessandria simply nodded.

"Lady Fireheart, the top left, Order of The Sacred Fire. Top Right Order of the Holy Water. But the bottom two are unknowns,"

Alessandria cocked her head. "Your family designed it?"

A whiff of intensely musty books made

Alessandria want to gag.

The Queen smiled. "I was only checking with you Lady Fireheart. I know history is more your Brother's area of expertise. The quarter with the leaf is the Order of the Blessed Earth,"

Alessandria rolled her eyes at the name. She hated that Order with a passion.

"The various lines and yellow background of the last quarter is something to do with the Noble Houses," Alessandria said.

The Queen smiled and nodded.

"Your majesty, I do not see why I am here,"

"Lady Fireheart, I need you to find out what the middle thing in the Coat of Arms is?"

Returning her attention to the Coat of Arms, Alessandria narrowed her eyes, and she could barely make out a little raised icon on the Coat. It was a curved triangular with the face of some kind of demon on it.

"I can barely see that. Why is it important?" Alessandria asked.

"Because Lady Fireheart, I fear it's a demon trapped inside the original Coat of Arms that the Triad wish to use against me,"

Alessandria stepped forward. "I cannot allow that. The Triad can't get any stronger,"

The Queen took her seat once again. "Excellent. The Records of the Coat of Arms including the design is inside the Church Office,"

Alessandria laughed at the Queen.

"Yes Lady Fireheart that is exactly why I need you. It looks far better for the House of Fireheart to attack the Church than me,"

"Well Daniel being a gay abomination does have its advantages," Alessandria said, walking towards the door.

As Alessandria left, the Queen shouted "It's in a large chest. Don't die!"

***

In all honesty, Alessandria couldn't believe the Queen had convinced her to attack or at least trespass on the Church. The almighty Organisation that controlled the people and made the Nobles hate her brother with a passion.

As Alessandria stepped into the stone hallway of the Church, she smiled and realised she had been wanting to do this for a while.

The stupid smell of cedarwood incense filled her senses and the taste of... something foul lingered in her mouth.

Wanting to get out of here as soon as possible, Alessandria looked up and down the long stone hallway. The cold yellow stone bricks neatly lined the hallway ahead of her.

Alessandria started to walk down the hallway, she wanted to spit at the horrible paintings of so-called saints and living gods. Daniel had given her a brief history lesson and all these men killed innocent people for their own pleasure and used their so-called divine power for dark purposes.

Of course Alessandria wasn't blind to the fact that the oppression of women, gays and children were acceptable back then. But in the name of the Gods, she wasn't so sure.

The feeling of the smooth stone floor reminded Alessandria to be careful. These floors were too smooth and too dangerous for her to be quick. One fall could give her present away.

The sounds of rather nice choirs echoed around the stone hallways. Alessandria knew they were here for evening practice that meant the priests and Vicars were busy for at least another hour.

Looking straight ahead, Alessandria saw a large oval wooden door. Its wood rough and black, and its iron cold and door handle unfriendly.

Reaching down to her waist, Alessandria went to grab her sword. But she had forgotten it. She swore under her breath. Typical she had been so caught up in the fact there was a lead on the Triad that she had forgotten her sword.

After a few more seconds, Alessandria was at the wooden door, she placed her fingers on the cold iron door handle. She turned it. It was locked.

Since when did Priests expect to be robbed? This was ridiculous. All she wanted was a simple design and some Priests locked a door.

Alessandria looked at the door. If she had her sword, she could easily pop the door open. But that was with her boyfriend. Damn him!

Looking around Alessandria saw the coast was clear and she thought about the morality of what she wanted to do. Breaking into a holy building. Was that right? It was for her Queen? Who was technically the official head of the Church.

That made it perfectly moral, right?

Before she could change her mind, Alessandria slammed into the door.

It didn't move.

Alessandria slammed again.

The sound echoed around.

The choir stopped.

Alessandria tensed.

The choir continued.

Alessandria slammed again.

The door cracked.

Footsteps echoed towards her.

Alessandria looked up the hallway.

Two long shadows were coming towards the hallway.

Alessandria smashed into the door.

The lock shattered.

Two men shouted.

Alessandria stormed inside.

She tried to shut the door. It was too damaged.

The men ran towards her.

Alessandria needed to be quick.

This entire office was pointless.

Scripture and relics littered the large room.

A brown desk laid at the back of the room.

Three massive stained glass windows were behind it.

Still no chest.

The men were getting closer.

Alessandria kept looking.

The stupid smell of incense grew stronger.

She looked to her left.

There was something large under a pile of scripture.

It looked like a chest.

Fists slammed into Alessandria's face.

She stumbled forward.

The two men were here.

She spun around.

Her fists up.

The two men whipped out their swords.

Alessandria frowned.

One man charged.

The other followed.

They swung their swords.

Alessandria dodged.

Rolling onto the floor.

The swords sliced into the stone floor.

Alessandria jumped up.

She smashed her fists into one man's face.

His jaw crunched.

He screamed in pain.

The other man swung his sword.

Alessandria grabbed the other man.

Pushing him in front.

The sword sliced into his chest.

Blood sprayed up the walls and floor.

The corpse fell to the ground.

Alessandria grabbed his sword.

She swung it wildly at the other foe.

Her swings were powerful.

The man could barely deflect them.

Alessandria jumped into the air.

Swinging her sword.

The man met her sword.

Alessandria kicked him in the head.

His neck snapped.

Alessandria didn't hesitate.

She rushed over to the pile of scripture.

Horrible text.

Alessandria pulled it away.

Revealing a massive red chest with a lock on it.

Taking a calming breath, Alessandria used her sword to pop the lock off and she opened it.

As air rushed out of the chest and Alessandria gagged as it stunk of dirty, musty parchment mixed with a large dose of sweat.

After recovering from the smell, Alessandria picked up a piece of yellow parchment with the symbol of the triangular demon from the Coat of Arms. There were some strange symbols and a dead language on the parchment. This would have to do.

More voices came from the hallway.

Alessandria had to move.

She placed the parchment in her pocket.

Alessandria needed a way out.

The windows.

Alessandria hated herself.

Even she didn't hate the Church that much.

She needed to survive.

She looked around.

Alessandria saw a massive chunk of gold.

The voices were getting closer.

Alessandria picked up the gold.

Throwing it at the stained windows.

They shattered.

Alessandria rushed over.

The guards close behind her.

Alessandria didn't have time to look.

She jumped out the window.

Slamming into a roof a few metres below.

Rolling carefully down the roof of the main church, Alessandria knew she had done her mission and hadn't been caught. Her Family's honour was intact (for a change).

***

As Alessandria walked out in the cold night air outside the Castle, the soft mud under her boots and the sound of guards talking all around her, she had to wonder why the Queen wanted the parchment.

Even when Alessandria had given it to the Queen, she didn't seem excited or nervous about the content. If anything she seemed happier to see Alessandria than anything else.

The smell of freshly roasted nuts made Alessandria smile and remember festival walks with her Father before he died.

Whatever the Queen truly wanted with the parchment that was a problem with another day. Alessandria knew her Queen was righteous and Just. If she wasn't Alessandria would have killed her by now. Anything to protect the people.

Then a memory came into Alessandria's mind a story as a child about the Creatures of Night (demons) and how they would attack the enemies of the Queen.

Alessandria shook her head. If that was true then she would only admire her friend's ambition.

Equally, Alessandria just wanted to be there to protect her. After everything the Queen had given her and her Family. Alessandria needed to return the favour.

But the threat from the Triad was tomorrow's problem. Right now, Alessandria wanted her boyfriend and most importantly her sword.

HEART OF THE REGENT

"The path to victory is never straight, but neither are you my son,"

-Harrison's Father

Feeling of the wonderful smooth wooden wheels of his wheelchair (and hearing the wood scrap across the stone floor), Harrison stopped as his eyes narrowed at the small stupidly tall wooden table in front of him.

He wanted to stand up and look at the maps on the table. He wanted, no needed to stand up and feel the supposedly hard cold cobblestone floor under his feet. That was all impossible now.

The bastard Triad with their damn explosion robbed him of all that, but Harrison would see them all burn. That was a promise.

Smelling the scent of oranges and something musty made him want to look around, and as he did Harrison shook his head as he saw all the piles of parchment, books and other objects related to his duty scattered around the stone chamber on lowered tables.

Despite most in the castle hating Harrison (For any reason. He was disabled? Gay? Autistic? All were good reasons) he had to admit the Queen had made sure her Regent was treated well.

In all honesty, Harrison had never known the Queen to be so fond of him. Sure, Harrison had helped her with treaties, military matters and more but that was him being him. He didn't want anything special. Another quirk of being autistic Harrison rarely knew what people thought, even his beautiful fiancée Daniel.

As much as Harrison wanted to think about his fingers running through his to be husband's long perfect hair and admire his beautiful movements and hair. Harrison knew he had his duty to complete.

Sure being Regent of Ordericous was an impressive title. Harrison was the first Regent in centuries, the first gay disabled one in Ordericous' history. Harrison willed the power of a monarch. But of course that didn't mean being Regent was perfect.

It was probably when the Queen ordered her Regent to sort out the military when Harrison realised his job was a blessing, and a curse. And that was what he was doing. Doing his job for the country and Queen (and boyfriend) he loved.

The sound of people walking and hearing multiple footsteps outside the stone chamber made Harrison frown. Walking. It's something everyone takes for granted. You never imagine you won't walk the next day or be more active in the night.

Harrison wanted to kick himself for these thoughts but he couldn't, clearly. He knew he kept telling Daniel he was okay and he had made his peace with not being able to walk. But what if he hadn't? What if he would grow bitter about it? What if…

So many questions ran through Harrison's mind. He didn't know any paralysed people and he didn't know how to deal with this too much.

Harrison remembered how moany and quite honestly a bully, he had been to Daniel for a week after the attack. He had said awful things, done even worse to the man he loved. But Harrison didn't know how to deal with it.

Paralysis is one thing but being autistic and not being able to communicate what you want clearly. That only makes things worse.

In the end, Harrison had finally realised and accepted his condition. But what surprised him more was Daniel still wanted to marry him. Daniel was still with him considering what Harrison had done to him. And that's why Harrison loved him. No matter what they had each other's back.

A loud knock at the door made him return his attention to the presence.

Harrison didn't even get to open his mouth before the heavy wooden door opened. Then a disgusting man walked in like he was King.

Just looking at this man was an assault on the eyes, not because he was unattractive but because the man showed off his wealth in the extreme.

Heavy expensive looking grey, black and red furs hang around his neck and back. Harrison supposed it was meant to be some sort of cape but it looked ridiculous.

Under all the silly furs, the man wore some kind of exotic armour. Maybe it was made from Troll hide but Harrison didn't know. Nor care. All he knew about Troll skin was in certain light their hide sparkled wonderfully. In battle though it was useless.

Stretching his neck to look at the man's face, Harrison was hardly impressed. The man's features were war hardened and rough for sure. It reminded Harrison of greasy sandpaper he used in the engineering department back in the day.

But those cold dead blue eyes made Harrison uncomfortable. Or the fact that the man was looking around for him annoyed him!

A part of Harrison wanted to cough to make this awful man look down but the smell of overpowering perfume coming from him was another good reason to cough.

After a few moments, the man caught Harrison (presumably out of the corner of his eye) and looked down at Harrison. Before rolling his eyes.

Harrison knew this was going to be a fun meeting, not.

"I presume you are the Regent," the man said, his voice harsh and dismissive.

"*Lord* Regent," Harrison said.

The man rolled his eyes. "Whatever you want to believe you are. I am Supreme Lord Commander Titus,"

Inside Harrison allowed a loud shriek of excitement to meet one of his heroes. This Titus was an impressive man, a Slayer of enemies and a saviour of the battlefield. He had more names and titles than most people in Ordericous' history.

On the outside, Harrison simply nodded.

"Lord Regent, why am I here? I have troops to train and then I have to deal with your *boyfriend*,"

Harrison wondered if the term boyfriend had ever been a swear word in Ordericous' past. For Titus definitely made it sound like one.

"You are here Commander because I will it. I am Lord Regent and I have the power to will it,"

Titus took a step back.

Harrison smiled. "The Queen has ordered you to aid the Procurators in suppressing the Church Riots and you have denied your Queen. Why?"

Titus cocked his head. "The Procurators are in charge of policing Ordericous. It is not the military's job,"

"It is when the Queen and the Lord Regent demand it," Harrison said.

"Little disabled gay, whatever power you think you have. You do not have it,"

For some strange reason, Harrison smiled. He wanted to fight this fight. For weeks he had been getting strange looks and whispers about him. But for the first time someone had challenged him directly. This was going to be fun!

"Little Titus, why do you think you are safe? You must know the Head of the Military position is… unsafe at best. It is a position the Queen uses to get rid of people,"

Titus stood firm.

"Now of course as Lord Regent I have power. I can help you keep your job for a little longer but-"

Titus shot forward.

Harrison tried to wheel away.

Titus grabbed the wheels of his wheelchair.

Harrison's eyes widened.

"You are nothing. You are just a little gay abomination pretending to have power. The Church will win and you will die," Titus said, pushing Harrison's wheelchair away.

Harrison hit his head on the wall when the wheelchair stopped. Titus walked away.

Of course Harrison had every right to declare Titus as a traitor and get the Procurators to arrest him. But that wouldn't be very fun, would it?

Anyway, Harrison smiled as he remembered what Titus had said or implied during this stupid talk. He was a supporter of the Church.

However, what was actually important was how he made it sound like the Church was going to war.

In reality, the Queen, Harrison and beautiful Daniel's family all knew the Church was planning something. Maybe Titus was the key to finding out what and who was behind it.

***

One amazing benefit of being a guy in a wheelchair is no one cares about you, and no one sees you. Or the more accurate description is no one wants to see you. Because then they feel sorry for you, and not caring about it is far easier.

Feeling the hard smooth wooden wheels against his cold fingers, Harrison rested his hands on the wheels in case he needed to move.

As he sat in a little corner of the large grey stone Shrine. The rough stone block walls were a cruel depiction of proper strong walls as it looked as if children had placed rocks on top of each other until they were high enough.

At least the black stone floor was better made with its slightly rough and bumpy texture. In a wheelchair, it felt as if something was vibrating as he moved.

The sound of pitiful religious singing and chanting echoed softly around the Shrine as the service started. Along with the smell of burning chocolate incense started to fill the Shrine as the vicar, or whatever he was, started to lit cylinder things. Maybe they were candles, but Harrison really didn't care.

Looking ahead, Harrison focused on the rows upon rows of rotten wooden benches where the poor, blind and paralysed sat or tried to. They all leaned forward. Presumably trying to get closer to the so-called Holiness of the vicar, and maybe he could cure them.

A part of Harrison liked the idea of a divine being, being able to heal everyone and make the paralysed able to walk once more.

In truth, Harrison knew this wasn't helpful. These people were all probably amazing, gifted and hard working. But their fixation with wanting to heal must have kept them back from achieving what they could in their new life.

Harrison wasn't blind to the fact that he had been extremely fortunate with his new paralysed life, but he didn't mean it was impossible for others.

But a group of five people in wheelchairs caught Harrison's eye as they weren't sitting forward or watching the Vicar. They were watching him and whispering amongst themselves. A threat to watch?

Returning his attention to the front of the Shrine, Harrison focused on the vicar as he was singing and preaching hate and disgusting anti-gay things to the masses. The vicar would die.

Then Harrison's eyes narrowed on Titus sitting

in the front row wearing a Holy white robe with two massive swords next to him. A wave of heat washed over Harrison. He knew he should have bought guards. Maybe he would in the future.

For now, Harrison listened to the disgraceful hate speech and breathed in the chocolatey incense until the singing stopped and Titus joined the vicar.

"Welcome, welcome mighty Worshipper Titus. A true hero of the Church, a hero of the Triad," the Vicar said, his voice ancient and ridden with disease.

Harrison smiled. This was exactly where he needed to be.

"It is my honour to serve the Triad. It is my duty to serve and take down the False Queen," Titus said.

"It is a pleasure to have you amongst our ranks. Please report on your meeting with the Gay Abomination,"

Harrison really wanted to laugh that that was his official name to the Triad. Surely three evil masterminds could create a better name for their enemies.

"It is as we feared. The gay disease has spread to the highest ranks of the Queen's Government. We must act. She must be killed,"

Harrison's face frowned. He wasn't enjoying this talk anymore.

"What does the Gay Abomination know about our righteous mission?" the Vicar asked.

The masses whispered fearful comments and more hate amongst themselves.

The group of five wheelchair users still whispered and looked at Harrison occasionally.

"Thankfully gay people still cannot think for

themselves so he only reported what the Queen said,"

Really!

Harrison's hands formed fists. That clown really said that?

Harrison was furious.

If he had legs, Harrison knew he would jump up and slaughter them all.

It was these religious zealots that weren't able to think for themselves.

It was them that needed to die!

Taking a deep calming breath, Harrison cleared his head. He needed to focus. All these zealots would die by a gay hand or not. They would all die in the end.

But he had to warn the Queen. The Queen was his priority. He had to fulfil his duty.

Harrison tried to carefully roll his wheelchair round so he would get to the exit behind him.

As he turned five armed men walked in. They grabbed Harrison's chair. Pulling him forward.

Fear gripped Harrison.

All eyes were looking at him.

Everyone sneered and looked at Harrison with disgust.

The group of five were silent.

Harrison needed a plan.

No guards. No weapons. No allies.

Just a wheelchair and his mind.

Harrison passed the blind, poor and paralysed and the Vicar came down to push him in front of the masses.

The Vicar threw Harrison to the ground.

The cold hard floor met his head.

Harrison managed to turn. Facing the Vicar,

Titus and the masses.

Titus smashed the wheelchair up.

Now Harrison was alone.

No guards. No weapons. No wheelchair. No allies.

Harrison needed to think but the Vicar stood in front of him before he could do anything.

"This!" the Vicar said, pointing down to Harrison. "Is what we fight against. This disease,"

Really? How stupid is this Vicar? What Harrison wouldn't give for a dagger about now.

The vicar whipped out a blade.

The masses cheered.

Harrison's eyes widened.

He searched his pockets.

No weapon.

Harrison wasn't impressed with himself.

The Vicar turned.

Pointing the blade at Harrison's throat.

This was not how he wanted to die.

Harrison needed to marry Daniel.

He needed to live.

Harrison threw his body sideways.

His lifeless legs slammed into the Vicar.

He fell.

Harrison crawled over to him.

The vicar punched him.

He thrusted the blade at Harrison.

Harrison grabbed the blade.

Titus kicked him in between the legs.

It didn't hurt.

The blade got closer.

The masses cheered.

"For the Queen!" someone shouted.
The vicar looked around.
Harrison didn't waste it.
He pushed his fingers into the vicar's eyes.
The vicar screamed.
His eyes popped.
Blood poured out.
Warm dark red blood covered Harrison.
He pushed the vicar's body to the ground.
Titus stormed over.
Harrison tensed.
Someone placed a dagger in Harrison's hand.
Harrison tried to look.
He didn't see who it was.
Titus swung his swords.
Harrison managed to roll over.
He dodged them.
Titus kicked him in the legs.
It didn't hurt.
Titus screamed.
He stomped Harrison in the stomach.
That hurt.
Titus swung his sword.
Titus' leg wasn't far away.
Harrison thrusted the blade into Titus' leg.
He released his sword.
Harrison rolled over.
Dodging the flying swords.
Titus hopped about.
Harrison rapidly crawled over.
He pulled out the blade.
He thrusted in again.
Titus screamed in agony.
Harrison pulled the blade out.

He kept slashing Titus' leg.
It was all he could reach.
Titus fell.
Harrison crawled over him.
Titus whacked him off.
He jumped on top of Harrison.
Slamming his fists in Harrison's face.
Harrison's face was on fire.
He felt the blade still in his hand.
Harrison went to slash Titus' throat.
Titus grabbed the blade.
Pressing it against Harrison's throat.
Titus' arm tensed.
A sword sliced off his head.
Titus' corpse thudded to the ground.

Five people stood in front of Titus. Harrison's eyes narrowed as he looked at each of them. He could have sworn these were the five from the group of wheelchair users earlier.

The man in the middle stepped forward.

"Lady Alessandria sends her regards," he said.

Harrison relaxed and allowed all tension in his body to leave. Trust his beautiful Daniel's sister to know where the Triad was and how to save Harrison.

The man kneed down and carefully asked Harrison:

"Lord Regent, is it okay if we carry you back to the castle? Or is that improper?"

Harrison turned to see all their wheelchairs were either destroyed or had corpses and brain matter on them.

"That will be proper on this occasion," Harrison said.

***

Sitting on one of the many random balconies in the castle and listening to the roar of the ocean waves in the distance, Harrison felt the warm hard metal chair pressing against his fingers. As Harrison knew he had to experience the world somehow as his lower body couldn't feel anymore.

Looking out over the utterly stunning country of Ordericous, breathing in the fresh salty sea air that left the taste of fresh fish on his tongue. Harrison smiled as he focused on the immense forests and the massive city in front of him. It was beautiful. There was nothing more that needed to be said about his country.

Harrison was Lord Regent. A sworn Protector, Servant and Warden of his Country.

To some that might sound horrific and extremely dull. And some days of course it was. But to Harrison, this was his life and he wouldn't have it any other way.

He loved his country with all his heart and Harrison would happily die defending it. Granted he wanted to get married to the stunning Daniel Fireheart first but Harrison would make Daniel, his Queen and most of all his country proud of him.

Harrison was never a fan of people making big deals because he was the first of a lot of things. But whether he liked it or not, Harrison knew he was the first Regent in centuries and the first gay disabled Regent in history.

To him, that meant Harrison was going to be the best Regent he could possibly be.

Even if that meant digging and carving out the corruption and the triad's influence in the Church.

As his father would say the path to victory was never straight. Of course, there would be a lot of challenges to come, but Harrison didn't mind things not being straight. In fact, he preferred them.

HEART OF THE STORY

"The Heart of the Story isn't obvious at first,"

-Procurator Times Editor

Cholea loved her job. It was the best job in the world. She knew her mother and father wanted her to be more like her brother and sisters who were actual Procurators protecting the innocent and hunting criminals. But Cholea loved her job.

And as she sat on a high grey metal bar stool with her young hands on the cool wooden bar, this was why she loved her job. As a Journalist for the Procurator Times, she didn't have to go out and hunt down the criminals, she only had to talk about them.

Breathing in the amazing scents of the rich posh perfumes in the bar, Cholea was in heaven. She had never smelt so many amazing smells before.

Spinning around on her barstool, Cholea tried to keep her excitement contained as she saw tens upon tens of the nobility and other notable figures walking about, sitting on the posh leather chairs and sofa. All with an expensive cocktail in their hand.

Just the idea of that was stunning to Cholea, she couldn't believe how these amazing people knew so much about cocktails to order one without looking at the menu.

Cholea remembered only minutes ago how an elderly Noblewoman had elegantly marched into the bar and said some weird cocktail name. Before saying she had no idea if it was a real drink. The nobility was making up words. How cool was that!

Taking another sweet perfumed breath, Cholea focused on making herself look good for this interview with one of the top Procurators in Ordericous. But as Cholea looked at her little black dress she seriously doubted she had any creditability in a place like this.

It also didn't help Cholea when she first got here she had studied the cocktail menu for a good five minutes and the rest of the Nobility watched her. Before an amazing woman, Lady Alessandria Fireheart, helped her by picking a drink for her.

Cholea shook her head as she thought about that. It was so embarrassing. A part of her didn't even know why she was here on this particular assignment. After all her editor had made it clear to her this was an important story. She couldn't fail. She could lose her job.

Spinning on her stool back to the bar, Cholea looked at her bright pink cocktail with a slice of pineapple on top. Cholea hadn't heard of pineapple before today. Picking it up and eating it, Cholea had no idea if pineapple was good or not. It had a weird sweet, sour taste.

"Jasper, I am looking for Cholea Times. Have you seen her?" a woman in a deep posh voice said to the stunning male bartender.

The bartender pointed in Cholea's direction and smiled at her. Before making the woman a strange green drink.

Turning to look at the woman, Cholea was stunned by how... well she looked considering she was over a hundred years old. Her skin was smooth and almost youthful. Even her dress was a long black silk one like a twenty year old would wear. But somehow this old lady managed to pull it off.

Standing up Cholea wasn't sure how you address an old female Procurator.

"Hello, I'm Cholea of The Procurator Times. It is a pleasure to meet you," Cholea said.

The woman smiled and sat on the barstool next to Cholea. Cholea smiled as she realised she had managed to get her to sit down.

"I must admit Cholea I was surprised to receive your interview request. Most people merely seek to serve me court summons,"

Cholea didn't know how to respond to that.

"I'm very sorry to hear that. Can I have your name please for the article?"

"Of course Cholea, I am Countess Ruby

Holdwell,"

Cholea cocked her head. She hadn't heard of a Countess before.

Ruby smiled. "My dear you are not the first person to be confused. A Countess is not legally part of the nobility and I have no powers nor land. It is merely a formality if the Queen wishes to reward someone without promoting them to the Nobility,"

Cholea nodded.

"And Countess scares the commoners so I have a little bit of power,"

Cholea nodded, unsure if she should write that down.

"What did you want to interview me about Cholea?"

"Countess, I wish for you to tell me about the event of the Crimson Killer nine decades ago. You would-"

"I know how old I was. It was my first case as a Procurator. Let me tell you the story,"

***

You see Cholea it was late winter in Ordericous when we started to find the bodies. Nine bodies so far but they were all young women with their special parts ripped into and their throats were slashed. There was a tenth male we found later on with his manhood ripped out.

Of course all of this was horrific and as a brand new Procurator I was certainly thrown into the deep end. I didn't know what to do at first.

As I said it was very late Winter when I was transferred the case and the tenth body of the male was found. Interestingly he was gay.

This was a very crucial piece in the case because the King before Last was actively hunting down gay people. So I theorised I was hunting down a person who supported the King. Since it was about that time when the King offered rewards for killing gays.

Disgusting I know.

So with that fact in mind, I went to the only logical place where the killer and a supporter of the King would go. The King's Club.

You wouldn't know it now because it was destroyed three winters later during some riots. They were fun to be a part of!

Anyway as I stood outside in the freezing cold snow with the snow falling heavily around me, my fingers felt like ice. My leather booted feet felt even worse as the black cobblestone road was covered in a thick layer of ice and snow.

It wasn't ideal.

Even the air was icy with all of my breath smelling of fresh air which coated my lungs with a thick layer of coldness. Breathing was rather scary in that weather. It's why a lot of people were told to stay at home. Travelling and being outside was far, far too dangerous.

As I looked through the snow which was becoming heavier and heavier with each passing minute, I saw the massive pillars outside of the cold red brick walls of the Club.

Now, you might be wondering why I was standing outside in the freezing cold and honestly you would be right to. But I was standing outside because I was waiting for an informant to come outside.

Yet at this point if my informant didn't come out soon, I was going to head off and come back tomorrow.

After a few moments and listening to the howl of the wind whip past me, I saw a little black side door open with a short teenage boy walk out shivering towards me. He was probably 16.

"Ya can't meet inside?" the teenage boy asked.

"I thought your masters wouldn't like a woman inside,"

"Na those jerks just want women to give birth and all that stuff,"

I shook my head at that comment. They were all horrible people inside.

"Has any member been missing or coming or going of late?"

"Yea miss, ya know that Justice-y guy,"

I nodded he was referring to the Lord Justice of the time which was in charge of the killing and fixing of the gays and foreigners.

The Lord Justice believed if you beat a gay for several hours a day you could beat the gay demon out of them. Of course they all tended to die by the end of the second hour.

To say I hated or found the Lord Justice a disgrace was an understatement. Which is why I fully supported our Queen when she decriminalised it.

But I have to admit the worse thing about the King's Club was even though they hated gays, women and foreigners. The teenage boy informant was being used by them all.

It was disgraceful.

"Thank you. Is the Lord Justice in there now?" I asked.

"Na miss. He gonna home,"

"Thank you. Take this," I said, passing him a dagger.

He nodded.

Now please keep that part off the record because of course he did kill all the members of the King's club that were abusing him. It was only eight people but they were raping him and six other boys and ten other girls.

I know a lot in the Procurators would call that illegal or not justice at all. But you didn't know these people like I did. Or how my body knew these people. It's why I became a Procurator because I wanted to stop these monsters.

I only wished I could have saved my sister. Life could have been very, very different.

A few hours later of investigating, standing by a fire and walking in the freezing cold snow, I managed to find the Lord Justice's House.

I'll admit it was stunning. It was a massive white marble creation the size of twenty football pitches, with about a hundred rooms and balconies. Just looking at it was an impressive sight.

The surrounding areas of the house smelt of sweet oranges from the rows upon rows of massive blood orange trees that grew around the property. Making it a default fence.

In all honesty, it wasn't so much the house I was interested in. It was the entrance to the house or the estate I wanted. Simply because I had seen the Lord Justice pop out on his horse. He would be back.

So I did what any Procurator would do who was breaking the rules and probably the law, I crouched behind a large bush of sweet-smelling flowers with my hands and feet pressing into the cold dry hard soil. No risk of footprints.

Looking ahead I saw a large black iron gate to the house locked and secured. No guards. No one was watching. I was just laying in wait.

After an hour, I heard a horse walk along the cobblestone road outside and stop in front of the gate.

Looking at the Lord Justice, I bit my lip. He was awful. His long elegant black silk robes of office and all his power he held in his hand. That he was using to kill and torture innocent women and gays. It was a disgrace to the Procurators.

As his well-aged hands took out the key for the

lock on the gate, I went for him.

I shot out.

Slamming my fists into his skull.

He screamed.

The horse fled.

He swore.

He called out names.

I couldn't hear them.

My fists slammed into him.

He slapped me.

He kicked me.

My stomach ached.

He whacked me.

I fell to the floor.

He called more names.

He thought I was gay.

Thinking I was the enemy.

He stomped on my stomach.

I grabbed his foot.

He kicked me.

Jumping on me.

He smashed my head into the cobblestones.

Blood wetted my hair.

He slapped me.

I needed to fight.

My body ached.

He bit my neck.

My body flooded with pain.

I punched him.

Knocking him off.

I jumped up.

He kicked my legs out under me.

He whipped out a knife.

Holding it against my throat.

He smiled.

He moved his hands below my stomach.

He wasn't doing that!

I screamed.

Three horses thundered down the road.

I slashed his face.

My nails sliced into him.

He moaned.

He enjoyed it.

I thrusted my nails into his ear.

He screamed.

I kicked him.

He flew off me.

Grabbing his head.

I smashed it into the road.

I smashed his head again.

And again.

His skull cracked.

Hearing someone cough, I looked up to see three tall women in long blue robes with the symbol of the Inquisition around their necks. I smiled to myself as I thought I was about to be killed by these all powerful Inquisitors which the law didn't apply to. They could easily kill me and nothing bad would happen to them.

***

By this point Cholea was leaning so far forward on her warm metal bar stool, she wondered if she could fall off.

Sitting back on the barstool and breathing all the sweet smelling perfumed air, Cholea smiled as she looked at Ruby. This amazing Procurator who had somehow survived the Inquisition. A very rare occurrence.

"How did you survive? What happened? They clearly didn't kill you?" Cholea asked.

Ruby smiled and took Cholea's hands. Cholea was surprised at how smooth and warm Ruby's well-aged hands were.

"They thanked me for doing their job for them and we all agreed to fake the report of what happened. Including what happened at the King's Club. Then the official report was sealed by the Inquisition,"

Cholea frowned and closed her notebook as Ruby said that. Cholea was so upset at that statement. She couldn't lose her job because she didn't have a job now. Cholea knew if something was sealed by the Inquisition it was suicide to write and print it. All of the Procurator Times would be destroyed.

Ruby rubbed Cholea's hands.

"Don't look so down," Ruby said.

"Why not I can't print this? Why even tell me?"

"Cholea, I like you. I'm over a hundred years old. I'm going to die soon. I suppose… I suppose I just wanted someone to know the truth. You are the only person in Ordericous that knows the truth,"

Cholea smiled at that.

"Thank you,"

"It was a pleasure meeting you," Ruby said, downing her drink and leaving.

Sitting on the barstool and watching Ruby elegantly walk out of there, Cholea was in slight amazement as she breathed in more of the sweet perfumed air, and listened to the talking of the nobility.

Cholea couldn't believe she had something no one else had. She had the truth of the Crimson Killer. And no one could take that away from her. No one.

Finishing the last of the delicious bright pink drink, Cholea remembered something about the true heart of the story that her editor had said when she first started. Surprisingly enough he was right, when Cholea walked here today she believed the heart of her story would be focused on the crime itself and why the killer did what he did.

In reality, the true heart of the story was something else and a lot more precious. Cholea smiled as she figured out the heart of the story was doing what's right and defending the good and innocent. Sure the teenage boy broke the law, but his actions saved himself and others from abuse. The same goes for the Countess.

Leaving her coins on the bar for her drink (and her business card for the hot barman), Cholea fell the bar smiling. Even if she lost her job, she would always find the true heart of the story. Because that's the best part.

GET YOUR FREE AND EXCLUSIVE SHORT STORY NOW! LEARN ABOUT NEMESIO'S PAST!

https://www.subscribepage.com/fireheart

https://www.subscribepage.com/psychologyboxset

Thank you for reading.

I hoped you enjoyed it.

If you want a FREE book and keep up to date about new books and project. Then please sign up for my newsletter at www.connorwhiteley.net/

Have a great day.

FIREHEART URBAN FANTASY SHORT STORIES COLLECTION

About the author:

Connor Whiteley is the author of over 30 books in the sci-fi fantasy, nonfiction psychology and books for writer's genre and he is a Human Branding Speaker and Consultant.

He is a passionate warhammer 40,000 reader, psychology student and author.

Who narrates his own audiobooks and he hosts The Psychology World Podcast.

All whilst studying Psychology at the University of Kent, England.

Also, he was a former Explorer Scout where he gave a speech to the Maltese President in August 2018 and he attended Prince Charles' 70th Birthday Party at Buckingham Palace in May 2018.

Plus, he is a self-confessed coffee lover!

OTHER SHORT STORIES BY CONNOR WHITELEY

Blade of The Emperor

Arbiter's Truth

The Bloodied Rose

Asmodia's Wrath

Heart of A Killer

Emissary of Blood

Computation of Battle

Old One's Wrath

Puppets and Masters

Ship of Plague

Interrogation

Sacrifice of the Soul

Heart of The Flesheater

Heart of The Regent

Heart of The Standing

Feline of The Lost

Heart of The Story

FIREHEART URBAN FANTASY SHORT STORIES COLLECTION

The Family Mailing Affair

Defining Criminality

The Martian Affair

A Cheating Affair

The Little Café Affair

Other books by Connor Whiteley:

The Fireheart Fantasy Series

Heart of Fire

Heart of Lies

Heart of Prophecy

Heart of Bones

Heart of Fate

The Garro Series- Fantasy/Sci-fi

GARRO: GALAXY'S END

GARRO: RISE OF THE ORDER

GARRO: END TIMES

GARRO: SHORT STORIES

GARRO: COLLECTION

GARRO: HERESY

GARRO: FAITHLESS

GARRO: DESTROYER OF WORLDS

GARRO: COLLECTIONS BOOK 4-6

GARRO: MISTRESS OF BLOOD

FIREHEART URBAN FANTASY SHORT STORIES COLLECTION

GARRO: BEACON OF HOPE

GARRO: END OF DAYS

Winter Series- Fantasy Trilogy Books

WINTER'S COMING

WINTER'S HUNT

WINTER'S REVENGE

WINTER'S DISSENSION

Miscellaneous:

THE ANGEL OF RETURN

THE ANGEL OF FREEDOM

CONNOR WHITELEY

All books in 'An Introductory Series':

BIOLOGICAL PSYCHOLOGY 3RD EDITION

COGNITIVE PSYCHOLOGY THIRD EDITION

SOCIAL PSYCHOLOGY- 3RD EDITION

ABNORMAL PSYCHOLOGY 3RD EDITION

PSYCHOLOGY OF RELATIONSHIPS- 3RD EDITION

DEVELOPMENTAL PSYCHOLOGY 3RD EDITION

HEALTH PSYCHOLOGY

RESEARCH IN PSYCHOLOGY

A GUIDE TO MENTAL HEALTH AND TREATMENT AROUND THE WORLD- A GLOBAL LOOK AT DEPRESSION

FORENSIC PSYCHOLOGY

THE FORENSIC PSYCHOLOGY OF THEFT, BURGLARY AND OTHER RIMES AGAINST PROPERTY

CRIMINAL PROFILING: A FORENSIC PSYCHOLOGY GUIDE TO FBI PROFILING AND GEOGRAPHICAL AND STATISTICAL PROFILING.

FIREHEART URBAN FANTASY SHORT STORIES COLLECTION

CLINICAL PSYCHOLOGY

FORMULATION IN PSYCHOTHERAPY

PERSONALITY PSYCHOLOGY AND INDIVIDUAL DIFFERENCES

CLINICAL PSYCHOLOGY REFLECTIONS VOLUME 1

CLINICAL PSYCHOLOGY REFLECTIONS VOLUME 2

www.ingramcontent.com/pod-product-compliance
Lightning Source LLC
LaVergne TN
LVHW021052100526
838202LV00083B/5831